For children everywhere.
Let your imagination grow
as without it we are just thinking.

"When I grow up,"
Charlie said.

"I will have a pet dinosaur,
and call him Ted."

"We will play out each day, in the rain or the sun."

"We will explore in the forest, it will be such fun."

"I will take Ted swimming.
"That will be so cool."

"Can you imagine a dinosaur in
the swimming pool?"

"Ted could be in my
football team,"

Charlie said with a grin.

"With Ted in goal, we would
surely win!!!"

"Ted could take me everywhere;
I would sit on his back."

"I would be safe with Ted, even
in the dark."

"Bathtime may be messy,"
Charlie Laughed.

"Have you ever seen a dinosaur
taking a bath?"

"I will share my breakfast...

lunch and tea with
Dinosaur Ted,
who will sit next
to me."

"Then at night, when it's time for bed, Ted will sleep in my room,"

Charlie said.

"We will read a story then at the stars we will peep"

"Until it's time to fall asleep."

sweet dreams...

Colour Ted

Charlie and Ted

ISBN

written by : Susan Carey

illustrated by : Alper Özdil

Text Copyright © 2022 Susan Carey
Illustrations Copyright © 2022 Alper Özdil

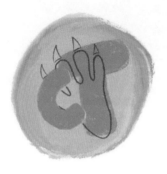

Printed in Great Britain
by Amazon

12392722R00016